Time Spies™

Where will they go next?

The postcard predicts
a most magical mission!

Magician in the Trunk

By Candice Ransom

Illustrated by Greg Call and Jim Bernardin

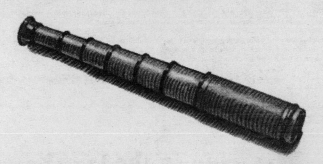

MIRRORSTONE

Cover and interior art by Greg Call and Jim Bernardin
First Printing: February 2007
Library of Congress Catalog Card Number: 2006937507

9 8 7 6 5 4 3 2 1

ISBN: 978-0-7869-4070-7
620-95610740-001-EN

U.S., CANADA,
ASIA, PACIFIC, & LATIN AMERICA
Wizards of the Coast, Inc.
P.O. Box 707
Renton, WA 98057-0707
+1-800-324-6496

EUROPEAN HEADQUARTERS
Hasbro UK Ltd
Caswell Way
Newport, Gwent NP9 0YH
Great Britain
Please keep this address for your records

Visit our website at **www.mirrorstonebooks.com**

To Nina,
my magical editor

Contents

Diamonds in the Sky

"I know something you don't know," Mattie Chapman said.

She and her brother Alex were in the back yard by the shed. They were looking for four-leafed clovers, though it was getting dark.

"I bet I know more than you know," said Alex.

Mattie opened the shed door. "Look."

A big box sat by the lawn mower. Red,

white, and blue letters said *Fireworks*.

"Cool!" Alex exclaimed. "Let's try one!"

A voice behind them said, "Not until the Fourth of July."

Mattie whirled to see her father. "But, Daddy, that's two whole weeks away!"

"I bought them for the Gray Horse Inn's Independence Day celebration," Mr. Chapman said. "We're going to have an old-fashioned fireworks show."

Earlier that summer Mattie's family had moved from a suburb in Maryland to an old house in Virginia. Not only was the house in the middle of nowhere, but her parents had turned it into a bed and breakfast. People slept in guest rooms and ate breakfast with them.

Mattie didn't think she'd like the old house. Then she and Alex and their little sister Sophie discovered the secret in the third floor tower. Now Mattie wouldn't live anywhere else.

"However," said Mr. Chapman, "you can have these now." He gave them each a small packet labeled *Diamond Sparklers*.

Mattie eagerly opened her packet and drew out a long, thin wire. She held it as her father lit the tip of the sparkler with his safety lighter. The sparkler hissed and sputtered.

Alex lit two sparklers off Mattie's and swooped them in double arcs.

"Look at me!" Five-year-old Sophie waved a sparkler from the porch steps.

A strange woman stood next to her.

"Let's write your name," the woman said to Sophie. Closing her own hand over Sophie's, she guided the sparkler.

"It's like diamonds!" Sophie cried. "Only in the sky!"

The woman helped Sophie finish her name with a flourish. "Bravo!"

"Gravy!" said Sophie.

Alex and Mattie giggled.

"Sophie, who's your friend?" Mattie asked.

"Her name is Ms. Pettibone-Shute," Sophie replied. "Guess what? She is staying in the Jefferson Suite!"

Mattie's heart leaped. A guest in the Jefferson Suite meant a new adventure! For some strange reason, only Travel Guides stayed in the special third floor suite.

"Tomorrow morning!" Mattie whispered to Alex. "We'll be off on a new adventure."

The next morning, Mattie hurried into the dining room ahead of Alex and Sophie.

Ms. Pettibone-Shute glanced up from buttering a muffin. "Good morning. Have one of these yummy Monticello muffins."

Mattie slid into the chair and helped herself to a muffin. "Daddy makes these from a really old recipe."

"They're named after Thomas Jefferson's

house," Alex said. "You should see Monticello. It's pretty close."

"I'm going there this morning to give a lecture on Jefferson's furnishings," Ms. Pettibone-Shute replied. "I'm an antiques dealer."

Across the table, Alex frowned. Mattie knew he didn't think selling old furniture was an exciting job.

Their first Travel Guide had been a Revolutionary War re-enactor. Mr. Jones sent them back in time to help George Washington at the Battle of Yorktown. Mattie loved their second travel guide, a paleontologist. Ms. Van Hoven sent them to a dinosaur dig in the 1890s. On their latest adventure, the kids climbed a beanstalk into the sky!

Alex tossed a nickel in the air. "Want to see a magic trick?"

"Ever since we saw this TV show about

magicians, Alex thinks he's Houdini," Mattie said to Ms. Pettibone-Shute.

"Ladeez and gentlemen. The Great Alexander—" He grinned. "Get it? Instead of Alexander the Great, I'm the Great Alexander."

Mattie rolled her eyes. Sometimes Alex acted like he was Sophie's age instead of eight, a year younger than Mattie.

"Get *on* with it," she said.

Alex ignored her. "The Great Alexander will now make this nickel disappear." He flicked the nickel over his index finger. Then he shifted it quickly to his left hand.

The coin fell to the table with a *clunk*.

His shoulders slumped. "I stink at magic.

"You'll get it," said Ms. Pettibone-Shute. "You never know who will help you."

Mattie exchanged a glance with Alex. Was their Travel Guide giving them a hint? None of them had ever *talked* about the adventure before it happened.

"Do you have postcards?" Ms. Pettibone-Shute asked. "I'd like to send one to my mother. She'd love to come to this inn."

Mattie jumped up and fetched a postcard from the sideboard. "If you put it in the silver tray, Mom or Dad will mail it."

Not really, she thought. Postcards written by the Travel Guides never got mailed. After the kids checked them, the postcards vanished.

Ms. Pettibone-Shute noted the photograph of Gray Horse Inn on the front.

"Nice picture," she said. "I'll tell Mother there are lots of antiques here. Like your interesting sideboard."

"What's so interesting about it?" asked Mattie.

"It reminds me of another sideboard I saw once." Ms. Pettibone-Shute scribbled a few lines, then put her pen down. "Furniture travels, you know. Just like people. If chairs and tables could talk, they would tell us amazing stories."

"Like fairy tales?" asked Sophie. She propped Ellsworth, her stuffed elephant, against the sugar bowl.

Mattie hoped not. Their last adventure involved Sophie's favorite fairy tale.

"More like mystery stories," replied Ms. Pettibone-Shute. "George and Martha Washington had a pair of matching sideboards in their home, Mount Vernon. Somehow one of the sideboards wound up at Monticello."

"Thomas Jefferson owned George Washington's furniture?" Alex said.

Ms. Pettibone-Shute leaned closer. "Here's the strange thing. The sideboard disappeared.

Years later it was found in West Virginia in a chicken coop! Chickens were roosting on it!"

Mattie laughed. "I think that sideboard would tell a funny story!"

"The story doesn't end there," said Ms. Pettibone-Shute. "The sideboard was displayed at the 1893 World's Fair."

"What's a World's Fair?" asked Alex.

"It's a big fair held every few years," Ms. Pettibone-Shute explained. "People come from all over to see new inventions and exhibits from countries around the world."

"Why didn't they just go to the Smithsonian museums?" Mattie asked.

"Not everyone could travel to Washington, D.C. People didn't always have television or even photographs. For a long time, the World's Fair was one of the only ways people could see the wonders of the world."

Ms. Pettibone-Shute stood up. "Well, I must get ready for my lecture." She dropped the postcard in the silver tray and left.

Mrs. Chapman bustled in from the kitchen and began collecting the plates.

"Bring the rest, please," she told the kids.

"Sure, Mom." Mattie watched her mother carry the dishes into the kitchen.

"Hurry!" said Alex.

Mattie sprang over to the sideboard and snatched up the postcard.

"What is it?" Alex took the postcard from her. "Not another castle! We went to one on our last trip."

"The postcard is only a hint. All the women have on long dresses," she said. "Good thing me and Soph are wearing sundresses today."

"What's the message?" Alex asked.

Mattie flipped the card over and read:

If we don't pack the house, we'll be home next week. —E.W.

"Who's E.W.?" Alex asked. "And how can you pack the house?"

"We won't find out until we're on our mission," Mattie reminded him. "Mom's coming! Clear the table, quick!"

They raced to gather plates and juice glasses. Alex dropped a coffee cup, but it didn't break.

"How will I ever be a magician?" he grumbled. "I've got butterfingers."

"He'll teach you how," said Sophie.

"Who will?" asked Mattie.

But Sophie had already run up the stairs, heading for the tower room. Mattie and Alex dashed after her.

Mattie pushed on the small two-shelf bookcase. It swiveled to reveal an opening into the tower room. She crawled through the opening, with Sophie and Alex right behind.

Tall windows covered three walls. The only piece of furniture, a desk, stood near the door.

Alex removed the brass spyglass from the secret compartment in the old desk and held it by one end.

"Wait," Mattie said. "Before we go, there's something we need to talk about."

Alex sighed. "What now?"

"I've been thinking about the rule," she said.

"What rule?" Sophie asked.

"The rule of time travel," Mattie explained. "About not changing history."

"Like when we go back in time," Alex prompted, "we shouldn't leave anything behind?"

"Right," Mattie said. "Or tell what's going to happen in the future. Or take anything home with us."

Sophie studied a threadbare spot on Ellsworth's head. She didn't say anything.

"I was thinking we should make a vow never to break the rule of time travel," Mattie said.

"I wouldn't say *never*," said Alex. "We can bend the rule if we have to."

Mattie shook her head. "It's our responsibility not to mess with history."

"Whatever you say." Alex lifted up the spyglass.

Sophie gripped the middle of the spyglass, clasping Ellsworth to her chest.

Mattie placed her hand on the other end and held her breath. She had never gotten used to this part.

"Spyglass!" Alex said grandly. "The Great Alexander commands you to take us away!"

Beneath Mattie's fingers, the brass cylinder grew warm. Stars and crescent moons appeared on the cylinder in blazing light. The spyglass began to vibrate.

Mattie closed her eyes. Her feet *whooshed* beneath her, as if the floor had dissolved.

Firecracker sparks in red, blue, and white—
lots of white—flecked behind her eyelids. The
sparkles spiraled, making her dizzy.

Then—*thump!*—her feet hit solid ground.

2

The Man in White

Mattie felt heat from the pavement through the soles of her sandals. At first she couldn't see anything but people. Men in round, black hats. Women in sweeping skirts.

Mattie felt like a rock in a stream.

"Alex!" she called. "Sophie!"

"Here!" Alex jumped up and waved. "Sophie is with me."

Mattie edged her way through the mob.

Alex and Sophie stood near an old-fashioned train that belched hot steam.

"Isn't it cool?" said Alex.

The train whistle shrieked. Sophie clapped her hands over her ears.

"Everyone's going that way," Mattie said, pointing toward the building.

"We should, too." Alex began wiggling between people.

Mattie grabbed Sophie's hand and followed. The sun was scorching.

Even though it was hot, she noticed all the men wore wool suits. Women's skirts dragged on the ground. Girls were dressed in shorter skirts and white stockings. Even boys had on short pants with black stockings.

Mattie figured she and Alex and Sophie looked a little strange, but not too much. At least nobody was staring at them.

Several wide archways divided the low building. People streamed through the archways. Mattie was carried along by the throng to a ticket booth.

Inside the glass window of the booth, a woman held out her hand.

"Day pass?" she asked Mattie.

Mattie started to say, "What's a day pass?" Then she felt something crinkle in her pocket—something that wasn't there before. She pulled out a large printed ticket.

Alex had a ticket in his pocket, too, but Sophie's pocket was empty.

Mattie handed the tickets to the woman. "How much for our sister? She's five."

"Children under six get in free." The woman punched the tickets and handed them back to Mattie. "Walk through the turnstiles. Next, please."

The kids pushed through a brass turnstile and entered a white paved plaza. In front of them stretched a rectangular pool as big as a lake. Its green water glinted like emeralds. Fountains spouted glistening jets of water high into the air. Dazzling white buildings surrounded the pool.

"We're in some kind of fancy city," said Mattie. "Like Oz."

Alex looked at his ticket. "It says, 'Admission to 1893 World's Columbian Expedition, Chicago.'"

"Ex*posi*tion, not expedition," Mattie said, reading her own ticket. "I think that means world's fair. Like Ms. Pettibone-Shute talked about."

"Oh, boy!" Alex danced around. "Where are the rides and games?"

"Not so fast," Mattie told him. "We need to figure out our mission."

Sophie picked up a colorful booklet. "That man dropped this."

Mattie took the booklet, but the man was immediately swallowed by the crowd.

"'Your Guide to the Columbian Exposition,'" she read. "It's a guidebook, with a map. Looks like we're in the Court of Honor."

"Does it say where the rides are?" Alex asked.

"Alex, be serious."

"Let's go there!" Alex pointed to the left of the fountain to an enormous white building only yards away. Wreaths and shields were carved along the top.

Mattie tipped her head back to read the words over the entrance. "Mining? Who cares about mining?"

"It sounds cool." In a few strides, he was halfway to the door.

Sighing, Mattie took Sophie's hand again. Sometimes Alex could be *such* a pain.

Inside, she gawked. They must be in the biggest building in the world. Maybe the entire universe! The ceiling went up and up, criss-crossed by steel girders. Light poured through glass panels. Their shoes pattered on the shiny marble floors.

The main gallery was lined with smaller buildings from different states and even different countries. The little buildings contained shelves of rocks. Rocks from France, rocks from Montana.

"Wow!" cried Alex. "Look at all this neat stuff!"

Bo-ring, Mattie thought. When they went to the Smithsonian, they saw things like the Hope Diamond. Who cared about plain old rocks?

Alex ran over to a replica of the Statue of Liberty carved from a white substance. "It's made of salt!" He pretended to lick the base.

Mattie waved in the direction of four guards in gold-braided uniforms and plumed helmets. "See those guys? Do you want to get us thrown out?"

"Relax," Alex said as they strolled down the hall. "You're supposed to have fun at a fair. I wonder if they have games in here."

Mattie stalked ahead, her sandals clipping on the gallery floor. Did Alex forget why they were sent here? Their mission wasn't going to walk up and announce itself. They needed to figure it out.

She reached the exhibit where the guards stood at attention. *South Africa-Kimberley Diamond Mines*, the plaque proclaimed.

Inside the exhibit booth, men in long robes rinsed ordinary-looking rocks in buckets of water. The dirt, Mattie noted, was *blue*.

She inched close to the brass divider rail. "Are those real diamonds?" she asked one of the workers.

"Yes, Miss," he replied. "After we wash, they are then cut."

Another man sat at a table covered with a dark cloth sprinkled with glitter. The man bent over a large whitish stone gripped in a clamp and carefully tapped a tiny chisel with a small hammer. A sliver of rock fell away, revealing diamond sparkle.

Alex and Sophie came up to the rail.

"What do you do with the crumbs?" Alex asked the diamond cutter.

"We save the diamond dust," the man replied. "Every part of the diamond is valuable."

"I thought it was glitter," said Mattie.

Several people approached, eager to watch the diamond cutter. A man dressed in a white suit and a white straw hat stood next to Mattie. He carried a silver-knobbed walking stick and leaned over the brass rail, staring intently at the stone.

A young couple paused next to Mattie. The woman's dress had puffed sleeves the size of soccer balls. A small drawstring bag hung on a belt around her waist.

Mattie stepped aside to let them see better.

"Oooh," the woman exclaimed. "I wonder how much that diamond costs?"

"If you want it," her husband said, "we'll have to sell the farm!"

"Oh, you!" She gave him a playful slap.

The man in the white suit stumbled against the rail. He caught himself with his walking stick.

"Are you all right?" Mattie asked him.

He mumbled, "Fine." Pulling the brim of his white straw hat over his eyes, he slipped out of the exhibit.

Mattie watched as he appeared to glide through the crowd. Then he was gone.

"Let's go," Alex said. "I want to find the rides."

As they left the South Africa building, Mattie heard the young woman cry, "My purse! It's gone!"

"It probably fell on the floor," the young man said. "We'll find it."

Mattie hoped they would find the woman's purse. They seemed nice.

Outside in the bright sunlight, they made their way down the white paved streets, alongside a lagoon with an island dotted with boats. Trees shaded the pavement, but it was still hot.

Mattie skimmed the guidebook as they walked. "It says the exposition marks the four hundredth anniversary of Columbus's voyage to the New World. And this is the biggest world's fair ever since they started having them."

"The buildings sure are big." Alex rattled off the names—Horticulture, Woman's, Fisheries.

At last they entered a neighborhood of narrow streets bordered by flower gardens. In their old neighborhood in Maryland, the houses looked mostly the same. But here, the houses were all different.

"Look, that house is a mansion," Mattie said. "But the one next door is a log cabin!"

"Who lives here?" Alex asked. "Are we still in the fair?"

Mattie consulted the guidebook. "The map says we're still in the fair."

They faced a white house with a red roof and a long porch. It seemed familiar.

"Mat, we've been here before!" Alex said. "Last summer."

"Mount Vernon!" Mattie said, recalling the family outing. "Where George and Martha

Washington lived. But that house was in Virginia, not Chicago."

"Maybe the place got moved or something," Alex said, stepping up on the porch.

"Welcome to the Virginia state building," a smiling woman greeted them. "This is an exact replica of Mount Vernon, home of the great George Washington."

"How come you didn't make a copy of Monticello?" Alex asked. "That's Thomas Jefferson's house. It's way more famous than Mount Vernon."

The guide's smile slipped. "Well! I'm sure you'll enjoy visiting your state's house."

"Each house around here is for a different state?" Mattie asked.

"Yes," the guide replied. "All forty-three are represented, plus the United States territories."

"Forty-three states?" Alex frowned. "But there's fif—"

"We'll take the tour now," Mattie said hastily, pushing Alex ahead of her.

Inside, she whispered, "It's 1893, remember? There must have been only forty-three states back then, not fifty."

The front hall was packed with curious tourists. People gazed at a life-size portrait of George Washington and at the colonial furniture.

"This mahogany sideboard," another guide announced, "which belonged to General Washington, was found as a hen's roost in West Virginia. It was restored and sent to our exhibit."

"That's the sideboard Ms. Pettibone-Shute talked about!" Alex said. He turned toward the guide. "Hey! You didn't say it was at Monticello!"

"Shh!" Mattie warned. "Do you suppose the sideboard has something to do with our mission?"

"I don't know. Let's see what's upstairs."

On the second floor they glanced at china pitchers and chairs and books belonging to other famous Virginians. Nothing very exciting.

Then Sophie said, "That was Thomas's." She stood on tiptoe in front of an opened book. A silver watch trailing a silver chain had been draped over the pages.

"Thomas who?" Mattie asked. She squinted at the name on the plaque. *Thomas Jefferson*.

She straightened up, catching a glimpse of white out of the corner of her eye. "Alex," she said. "Jefferson's stuff is here."

"I know. Look!" He pointed to a brass spyglass propped in a brass tripod.

Mattie let out a slow breath. "That's the spyglass we saw in Monticello. They must have let the fair people borrow it."

"It's just like ours," Alex said. He pulled their spyglass from one of his pockets. "See? Same size. Same kind of metal. Same everything."

"I wonder if Jefferson's spyglass is magic."

Alex sidled up to the table. "We could try it," he said in a low voice. "At least we can touch the spyglass here. When we were at Monticello, we couldn't get near it."

Mattie chewed a strand of hair. Should they? What would happen if it turned out Jefferson's spyglass was magic, too?

Sophie tugged on her skirt. "Can I have a Coke? I'm thirsty."

"I don't know if they have Coke here,"

Mattie said. "But they must sell cold drinks."

"What about T.J.'s spyglass?" Alex asked.

"We can always come back." Secretly, Mattie was relieved Sophie wanted a drink. She felt funny about testing Thomas Jefferson's spyglass.

As they trooped downstairs, the hair on the back of Mattie's neck prickled. She twisted around, thinking they were being watched. Tourists flowed up and down the staircase like ants at a picnic. She thought she saw a flash of white again, but it disappeared in the mass of people.

At that moment, someone yelled in a raspy voice, "Stop those kids!"

What kids? Mattie wondered.

"Those kids are stealing Thomas Jefferson's telescope!" the voice shouted. "Call the guards!"

Mattie couldn't see who was yelling. Then she realized Alex still held their spyglass in his hand. Somebody thought they had swiped the spyglass from the Jefferson exhibit!

Another man took up the cry. "Grab those kids! They've got Jefferson's spyglass!"

"Run!" Mattie shouted.

They pelted down the steps.

Tweet! Tweeeet!

A shrill whistle cut through the air. Two burly uniformed guards ran toward them.

3

Real Magic?

"Stop! Thief!" shouted one of the guards. The men chased the kids into the street.

Mattie darted in and out among the tourists like a skateboarder. Sophie and Alex were right behind her. They raced down a long street beside a duck pond. Mattie could hear the policemen huffing and puffing several yards behind.

A wide arch loomed ahead, topped with a sign that read *Midway Plaisance*. People swarmed through the entrance.

Mattie didn't know what the words meant, but they needed a place to escape.

"This way!" she said, making a sharp right. Alex and Sophie followed.

Mattie didn't think it was possible, but more tourists than ever thronged the avenue. She and Alex and Sophie jogged down a wide street lined with fruit trees and evergreens, dodging sightseers.

At last Mattie dared to look back. The guards were gone.

"We lost them," she said, slowing. Then she noticed Alex still had their spyglass in his hand. "Do you want to get us arrested? Put that away!"

"I forgot it was in my hand," he said sheepishly. He shoved the spyglass in one of his pockets.

Mattie glanced around. Down the street, a row of thatched cottages rose behind a stone castle. The sign said, *Irish Village*.

"Where are we?" asked Alex.

Mattie unfolded the map. "This is called the Midway. I guess this part of the fair is like Olde Country Playworld. You know, with pretend countries like Scotland and France?"

"Yeah! And rides like the Loch Ness Monster roller coaster!" Alex said. "Where *are* the rides?"

"There." Sophie pointed up.

Mattie gasped. Soaring overhead was the biggest Ferris wheel she had ever seen. Instead of puny two-passenger seats, this Ferris wheel had dozens of compartments as big as train cars.

"Wow! Now *that's* a monster!" Alex sprinted in the direction of the Ferris wheel.

Mattie and Sophie hustled after him, passing Java Village and an ostrich farm. When they caught up to Alex, he stood before a gate. *Ferris Wheel Admission, 50 cents.*

"I thought it would be free," he said, disappointed. "Like at Olde Country Playworld."

"I guess our ticket only works in the part with all the buildings," Mattie told him. "Here we have to pay."

"I've got my allowance." He thrust his hand in his pocket.

Mattie shook her head. "You can't use our money. It's different. The ticket guy will think it's counterfeit."

He glared at her. "Why are we *here* if we can't have any fun? I wish we'd never come on this stupid trip!" Without another word, he ran off.

She sighed. "Come on, Soph. Who knows

what trouble he'll get into next."

They found Alex in front of a building called Kohl and Middleton Dime Museum. A poster advertised fantastic acts. *Electric Girl! The Human Claw-Hammer! The Nail King! Sampson, the Strongest Man on Two Continents! The Brothers Houdini!*

A hawk-eyed man paced on a platform, calling out to people passing by. A boy about Alex's age crept along one side of the platform.

"Step right up, folks!" the sharp-eyed man shouted. "Come inside and see the most amazing sights in the world! One thin dime, one tenth of one dollar—a *steal*, ladies and gentlemen—for a once-in-a-lifetime experience!"

"Mattie!" Alex exclaimed. "Houdini is performing! Remember the TV show? The Handcuff King!"

Mattie stared at the poster. "It says the Houdini *Brothers*. I don't remember any brother."

"It has to be Harry Houdini," Alex insisted. "*Houdini*! The greatest magician ever!"

"We don't have any 1893 money, Alex." Mattie knew the sharp-eyed ticket-seller would spot their modern money in an instant.

A couple walked up to the platform. The man took their money and peeled two tickets off a roll. While he was busy, the boy slipped inside the museum.

Alex whirled, wide-eyed. "Did you see that? That kid just snuck in! We can, too!"

"No, we can't!" Mattie said. "It's—it's not responsible."

"I'd pay but you won't *let* me." Alex sidled over to the entrance.

"Alex—!"

Alex boldly sneaked inside. Mattie held her breath as she shoved Sophie ahead of her through the door. She expected the hawk-eyed man or the customers to yell at them.

But no one did.

Inside, Mattie waited a few seconds for her eyes to adjust to the dimness. She expected rows of exhibits and display cases like other museums. Instead, a long hallway led to a pair of heavy doors.

"Funny museum," she whispered to Alex. "There's nothing to see."

"Maybe the stuff is in that room," said Alex.

The doors opened and a group of men smoking cigars came out.

One of the men remarked, "What a lousy show. Who couldn't lift an anvil?"

Another puffed on his cigar. "Waste of a

dime. Those magicians probably aren't any better."

Mattie wrinkled her nose as she walked through the cloud of cigar smoke. "Phew!"

The room turned out to be a theater with rows of red velvet plush seats slanting down to a stage. Red velvet curtains were drawn across the stage. To the far right, a brass easel held a card that announced, *Sampson! Strongest Man on Two Continents!*

A girl in a green silk dress removed the *Sampson* card and put another in its place. *Houdini Brothers! Modern Monarchs of Mystery!*

"The Houdini Brothers are next!" Alex said. "Quick! Find seats."

The theater wasn't even half full. The kids easily found three seats together near the front just as the lights went down.

The red velvet curtains rose to reveal two men, one tall and one short, dressed in black suits. They stood on either side of a large, black-painted cabinet, curtained in black. The cabinet reminded Mattie of the wardrobe in her parent's bedroom.

A large wooden trunk on wheels squatted before the cabinet. In front of the trunk, a padlock, rope, and other objects were spread on a blue cloth.

"I wonder which guy is Harry Houdini?" Alex asked.

The shorter of the two men stepped forward. "Welcome to our show, ladies and gentlemen. My name is Harry Houdini and this is my brother Theo."

Mattie studied the short man. He had wavy dark brown hair and strange gray eyes. She couldn't look away from those eyes.

"Prepare to be amazed!" Harry Houdini said.

"To begin," Theo said, stepping forward. "I need three volunteers—"

"Me! Me!" Alex waved his hand wildly and leaped up. "Pick me! Please!"

Mattie was sure he would be called. No one was jumping up and down like her brother.

But Theo's gaze swept over Alex. He chose two men and a woman. The men wore black suits and the woman's dress was black.

"Please come onstage," Theo asked the volunteers. "And examine our props."

The volunteers inspected the items on the blue cloth—a padlock, tape, rope and a stick of wax. They peered into the sack and thumped the sides of the trunk and cabinet.

"No secret panels," said one of the men.

Harry put the bag in the trunk and climbed inside it, pulling the top of the bag over his head.

"Would you please tie the bag?" Theo asked the volunteers. They tied the bag shut.

Then Harry knelt in the trunk. The volunteers closed the trunk, padlocked the lid, and bound the trunk with rope. Theo rolled the trunk into the cabinet.

"Ladies and gentlemen," Theo said dramatically. "I shall clap my hands three times. At the third and last time I ask you to watch closely for—the *effect*."

He clapped three times. Then he entered the cabinet and swung the curtain shut.

Almost instantly, the curtain opened again.

Mattie stared in disbelief.

Harry Houdini struck a dramatic pose in

the cabinet doorway! His gray eyes glittered in triumph.

"Cool!" Alex exclaimed.

The volunteers rushed forward to untie the ropes, unlock the padlock, and lift the lid of the trunk. The sack-covered shape inside wobbled to a standing position. The volunteers ripped off the wax seal and cried out as a head and shoulders appeared.

It was Theo! He shucked the sack and hopped out of the trunk. Both magicians bowed to scattered applause. Some people, Mattie noticed, were asleep.

Alex clapped so hard, Mattie was afraid he'd bruise his hands.

The velvet curtain dropped and the girl in the green dress came out to change the card.

"That was the best!" Alex said. "Let's go

backstage. Maybe we can meet them."

They followed the girl in the green dress down a narrow hallway. Performers sat in groups in tiny dressing rooms, eating and playing cards.

The Houdini brothers were talking to a man in trunks and tights. Mattie figured he was Sampson, the strongest man on two continents.

Harry Houdini's gray eyes fixed on them. "What have we here?"

"We saw your show," said Mattie. "My brother wanted to meet you. If that's okay."

"You were great!" Alex gushed to Harry. "I want to be a magician just like you!"

"Do you really?" Harry smiled. "What's your specialty?"

"Uh—coin tricks," Alex said. "What you just did out there . . . was that *real* magic?"

"That was real technique," Harry replied. "I keep people's eyes on one thing while I do another. It's called misdirection."

"Oh. I thought your magic was real."

"Where are your parents?" Harry asked them.

"They're, uh—not too far from here," said Mattie.

Theo ducked into their dressing room, returning with a paper sack. "Try some of this. It's a brand-new food, introduced here at the Fair."

Mattie reached into the bag and scooped out a handful of molasses-covered popcorn. "It's like Cracker Jack," she said in surprise.

"Can you help me with my coin trick?" Alex asked Harry.

"Sure, kid. Give me a coin."

Mattie drew in a breath. Alex was going to

show Harry Houdini modern money!

Before she could stop him, Alex dug out a large, silver coin. An eagle was inscribed on the back. And the year, 1893!

"A new silver dollar." Harry tossed the coin, then slid it from behind Ellsworth's ear.

Sophie giggled.

Harry showed Alex how to make the coin disappear. When Alex finally did it right, Harry clapped him on the back.

"Be careful with your money," he warned them. "There are a lot of thieves out there."

Theo yawned. "I didn't sleep that well last night. I'm going to catch a nap before our next show."

"You have another show today?" Mattie asked.

"Five," answered Harry as Theo closed their dressing room door. "We perform our act twelve times a day."

"Wow!" said Alex. "You guys work hard."

"It wouldn't be so bad if people came. I thought we'd draw big crowds at the Fair."

"We'll come to every show," Alex promised.

"Thanks, kids." Harry sighed. "Sometimes I wonder if I'm cut out to be a magician. If business doesn't pick up, my brother and I will have to go back to New York."

Like pulling a rabbit out of a hat, Mattie suddenly knew their mission.

— 4 —

The Show Must Go On

"Go see the amazing Houdini Brothers!" Mattie announced. "The greatest magicians ever!"

"Next show is at eleven-thirty!" Alex said in a booming voice.

"Better than this dumb old balloon ride!" Sophie added.

When they left the Museum, Mattie told Alex and Sophie she had figured out their mission. They had been sent to the World's

Fair to drum up business for the struggling Houdini Brothers.

"We need to tell people to go see the Houdini Brothers show," she said. "So they won't leave."

The kids stationed themselves next to the Captive Balloon. For two dollars, people could go up in a hot air balloon tied to a 1500-foot-long rope. Mattie had noticed the ride attracted lots of people and it wasn't far from Kohl and Middleton's Dime Museum. It was the perfect spot to tell people about the Houdini show.

"Forget the balloon," she called. "Go see the Houdinis!"

"Hey!" An angry man in baggy checked pants rushed toward them. "What are you tryin' to do? Scare off my customers? Get away!"

Afraid he might call the guards, Mattie

herded the others down the street. They couldn't help the Houdini Brothers if they were in jail!

"How about if we stand here?" Alex pointed to the Ice Railway. "Look at all the people. Everybody wants to ride this."

Kids and grown-ups shrieked in giant sleds that whizzed along a snow-covered track. Snow machines kept the track frozen even in the summer sun.

"Ellsworth is tired." Sophie plunked herself down on the ground. "We want to ride on a sled."

"Soph, we can't," Mattie said. "We have to help Harry."

"I want to go on the sled." Sophie stuck out her bottom lip.

Mattie took one of her arms. "Sophie, you can't."

"WANT TO SLEDDDDDD!"

Mattie threw Alex a desperate glance. Sophie hardly ever pitched a fit. But when she did, her tantrums made headlines.

"Get *up*, Sophie!" Mattie whispered. "People will think you're a big baby."

A couple standing in line turned to stare at them. "Little children should be left to be cared for in the Children's Building," the woman said loudly.

"SLEDDDDD!" Sophie wailed.

"D*o* something!" Mattie said to Alex.

He took a coin from his pocket. "Hey, Soph! Watch this! I'll make the nickel disappear."

Alex held the nickel in his right hand in front of Sophie's nose. Then he pretended to pass it to his left hand. He opened his empty left hand, then his right, revealing the coin.

Sophie sniffled. "Do it again!"

Alex performed the trick again, opening his right hand with a flourish.

"Aren't you clever!" the woman in line said. "How did you do that?"

Mattie stepped up. "Harry Houdini showed him. He's a famous magician. Go see the Houdini Brothers show at the Dime Museum. It's great!"

Alex did the trick a few more times. Soon a crowd gathered around him. Mattie pointed the way to the Dime Museum ticket booth. The crowd headed for the Museum's double doors.

"The Houdini brothers will be happy," said Alex. "Let's go backstage and tell them."

They found Harry Houdini pacing in the hall outside the dressing room.

"Theo is sick. Too much popcorn," he told them, running his fingers through his thick, wavy hair. "We go on in twenty minutes. I need a partner!"

Alex waved his arm like he was flagging down a bus. "Me! I'll do it!"

Harry smiled at him. "You'd be terrific in the act, Alex, but I need somebody a little bigger." His gray eyes fell on Mattie. "You're just the right size."

"M-me?" she stammered. "I don't think so."

"C'mon, Mat," said Alex. "You know what they say—the show must go on!"

"It's really easy," Harry said.

Mattie felt like she'd swallowed an ice cube. "What if I mess up? In first grade I was supposed to sing 'My Favorite Things' in the school play. When I opened my mouth, the only thing that came out was this little croak."

Harry laughed. "You won't have to sing."

"Okay," Mattie said. "I'll do it." They *were* supposed to help Harry Houdini.

Harry stared at her sundress. "Your frock is pretty but a little odd. Let's see if we can get you a costume. Georgia!"

The woman who changed the cards on the easel hurried down the hall. "Yes?"

"Can you find something for Miss Mattie to wear? She's taking Theo's place in the next performance."

"Come with me." In Georgia's dressing room, she took a black satin dress off a peg. "Try this."

Mattie ducked behind a folding screen to change. Her shaking fingers couldn't fasten the slippery buttons.

"Let me." Georgia finished buttoning the dress.

Mattie could barely breathe! How did girls

ever do anything back in the old days?

"You look very nice," Harry said when Mattie returned. Then he recited the opening lines, telling Mattie what she was supposed to say and do.

Ladeez and gentlemen, Mattie thought, in a daze. *The Great Alexander—* No, that was Alex's introduction.

Sophie and Ellsworth sat on the trunk. Alex bounced in and out of the black-painted cabinet, flapping the black curtain. Two men and a woman, all wearing black, leaned against the wall by the stage entrance.

"Now," said Harry. "When you call for volunteers from the audience, pick Evan, Stan, and Maria." The group by the entrance smiled at Mattie.

"Those are the same people Theo picked," Mattie said.

Harry nodded. "They're part of the act. After you call them up, they will inspect the props. Then you say the cue lines."

"What are they?" Mattie asked.

Harry held one hand out dramatically. "Ladies and gentlemen. I shall clap my hands three times. On the third and last clap, I invite you to watch closely for—the *effect!*' That's my cue."

"The *effect*," Mattie echoed. "Okay. I think I have it."

"Don't worry about switching as fast as Theo does," Harry told her.

Switching *what*? Mattie began to sweat. Harry hadn't told her how to do the trick.

"That's Sampson's applause," Harry said. "All right, everyone, it's show time."

The "volunteers" had left to find seats in the audience. A couple of assistants wheeled the black cabinet on the stage. Harry came behind, rolling the trunk. He opened the lid and spread out the blue cloth, laying the tape, padlock, wax, and rope on it.

Georgia waited until everything was in place, then went out front to change the card on the easel.

Harry stood on one side of the cabinet, looking mysterious. Mattie took her position on the other side, a fake smile pasted on her face. Her heart hammered so loud, she was sure everyone at the Fair could hear it.

The red velvet curtain opened. Mattie squinted past the glaring stage lights into the theater. People's faces looked like blobs. How would she pick out the three volunteers?

"You're on!" Harry whispered.

Mattie stepped forward. "Er—ladies and gentlemen—"

"Louder!" someone yelled.

"Ladies and gentlemen!" she announced. "Welcome to our show. Prepare to be amazed. First—"

The same guy shouted, "I thought this was the Houdini *Brothers*? Who's that girl?"

Harry gave the heckler a searing look. "Theo Houdini, my brother, is indisposed. But our lovely little sister, Mattie, agreed to take his place."

Mattie gulped. Now she was supposed to be Harry Houdini's sister!

"Uh—" She had lost her place in her speech and had to start over. "Welcome to our show. Prepare to be amazed. First, I will need three volunteers from the audience."

Hands shot up, including the heckler's. Mattie pretended to consider everyone, but pointed to Evan, Stan, and Maria.

"Please come onstage and inspect our props," she said. The volunteers came up and checked the props.

Harry Houdini placed the sack in the trunk and climbed inside, as before. The volunteers secured the top and sealed it with wax. They closed the lid, padlocked it, and bound the trunk with rope. Then one of the men wheeled the trunk into the cabinet.

Mattie could hardly see them as they worked. Their dark clothes blended with the black-painted cabinet.

Mattie looked at the audience, then spoke clearly, "Ladies and gentlemen. I shall clap three times. On my third and final clap, I ask you to watch for"—she paused—"for the *effect*!"

Her palms were slick as she clapped. She still didn't know how the trick worked! Harry said not to worry, but she *was* worried.

Then she slipped behind the black curtain of the cabinet and drew it shut. Instantly, hands jerked her backward.

"In here!" Harry whispered, pushing her into a trapdoor cleverly built into one end of the trunk. A second bag lay inside.

Harry helped Mattie climb into the bag,

then pulled it over her head. She felt him tie the top. Then he was gone. It was over before she had a chance to breathe!

Oohs and ahhs from the audience told her Harry had appeared in the doorway of the cabinet. Next she heard the volunteers yanking off the ropes and then the creak of the trunk lid being lifted.

Heart pounding, Mattie felt the volunteers rip the wax seal and open the top of the cloth sack.

On trembling legs, she stood up. Harry helped her out of the trunk.

Applause rang throughout the theater. Even the heckler whistled and cheered.

Mattie took her bow with Harry Houdini. The audience clapped even harder.

Several people surged up on the stage. A woman gave Mattie tickets for free ice cream.

"You are so brave," the woman said.

"Thank you." Mattie didn't feel brave. She was glad it was over!

After Mattie changed back into her own clothes, Harry invited the kids back to his dressing room. Theo was awake and sitting up on his cot.

"You'd better get out of that bed," Harry told his brother. "Mattie might put you out of a job. The crowd loved her!"

"Crowd?" Theo said.

"These kids drummed up business for us," Harry said. "The theater was more than half full."

Alex was examining the trapdoor on the side of the trunk. "Cool. How did you think up a trick like this?"

"I didn't. I bought the act for twenty-five dollars."

"How can you buy a trick?" Mattie asked.

"Another magician needed money. He sold me the trunk and the cabinet. And the secret to make the trick work." Harry grinned. "Can anybody guess what it is?"

"Them," Sophie said, pointing to the volunteers.

"Right! Because my assistants wear black, they move almost invisibly in front of the cabinet," Harry replied. "The audience was busy watching Mattie. They didn't see Maria drop an identical black sack inside the cabinet."

"How did you get out so fast?" asked Alex.

"Practice," Harry replied. "When Theo does the act, we actually change places using the same sack. But because this was Mattie's first time, I used a second sack."

"Your next show is at one-thirty," Alex said,

checking the schedule on the door.

"I bet you have even more people."

Mattie held up her tickets. "Look what somebody gave me. Let's get some ice cream and come back for the next show."

They went next door to the Vienna Café.

"I want peanut butter chocolate chip mint," Sophie said to the waiter.

The young man looked confused. "I'm sorry, Miss. We only have vanilla."

"I like our time better," Alex whispered to Mattie. "We have more ice cream flavors." But his eyes grew round when he saw the fancy glass goblets, piled with snowy scoops.

When they returned to the Dime Museum, Mattie was shocked to see only a handful of people in the theater.

The kids ran backstage. Harry and Theo stared at the floor, dejected.

"We'll rustle up more people," Alex promised.

Harry flashed a ghost of a smile. "Audiences are fickle. One minute they love you. The next, they don't. Oh, well, Theo and I can always go back to New York."

"Don't do that!" Alex said. "Maybe—*maybe* you need to put something else in your act."

"Like what?" asked Harry.

Mattie clenched her fists. *No, Alex!*

Before she could stop him, Alex blurted, "How about something with handcuffs? You could call yourself—I don't know. The Handcuff King?"

Mattie couldn't believe her ears. Her blabber-mouthed brother had just broken the Number One Rule of time travel!

5

The Jefferson Thief

Mattie grabbed Alex's arm. "I just remembered—we have to meet our parents." She hustled Alex and Sophie out of the museum.

"Wait a minute!" Alex protested.

"Are you *crazy*?" she said, storming down the street. "You told Harry Houdini what he was going to be in the future!"

"I was just trying to help."

"That could mess up Harry's life forever!"

"I don't even think he heard me," Alex said. "He didn't say anything."

Mattie sighed. "Promise me you won't do it again."

A brisk breeze rippled through the Midway. The wind slapped a sheet of paper across Mattie's leg.

"Hey," said Alex. "The Fair has its own newspaper. Hold still, Mat, I want to read the comics."

"Ha-ha." Mattie pulled off the newspaper. She was about to wad it up when she noticed something.

"What?" Sophie asked.

Mattie pointed to an article, "Jefferson Thieves Raid Mount Vernon."

Alex leaned closer. "What does it say?"

"It says Thomas Jefferson's watch was stolen from the Virginia state house earlier today. And somebody saw three children running from the scene of the crime." Mattie looked up. "They mean us!"

"But we didn't take anything," Sophie said.

"Relax," Alex said. "Even if the police catch us and lock us up in jail, we can get out."

Mattie made a face. "How? With one of your magic tricks?"

"With our secret weapon," Alex reminded her. "The good old spyglass."

"It doesn't matter." Mattie stabbed the newspaper article with her finger. "It's written down that three kids—us—may have stolen Jefferson's watch. We're part of the history of this fair. *And we're not supposed to change history!*"

Alex shrugged. "Okay, okay! The handcuff thing just slipped out."

Mattie tucked her hair behind one ear. "Now we have two missions. Help make Harry

Houdini famous. And clear our name. We just have to figure out how."

"First we'll find the real thief," said Alex. "Shouldn't be too hard—there's only about a gazillion people here."

Mattie stared down the Midway. Alex was right. The street swarmed with people. Just ahead of them, a woman stood in line for the captive balloon. The curling white feather on her hat bobbed in the breeze.

Mattie stared at the woman's hat. The white feather reminded her of something.

"That man looking at the diamonds," said Sophie quietly.

Mattie snapped her fingers. "That's it! Alex! Remember that guy at the diamond display? All in white?"

"Yeah. What about him?"

"I think he was in Mount Vernon when

we were there," said Mattie. "I saw something white. I think he's the one who yelled for the guards. And remember at the diamond exhibit? He stumbled—"

"And then that lady said her purse was gone!" Alex said.

"I bet he stole her purse!" Mattie said. "Then at Mount Vernon, when he yelled for the guards? He knew we didn't steal the spyglass. It was just a distraction, so everyone would be looking at us while he stole the watch."

"The dirty rat pinned the job on us." Alex talked out of the side of his mouth like a gangster in an old movie.

"Well, he's not getting away with it!" Mattie stuffed the newspaper into a nearby trashcan. "Let's take that old-fashioned Metro back to the main part of the Fair. We might see him again."

If they did, Mattie wasn't sure what they would do. Try to wring a confession out of him? Now she was thinking like Alex.

The Intramural railroad wasn't as fast as the Metro the kids once took in Washington, D.C. But it only cost ten cents and Mattie was glad they didn't have to hike across the park. When the train stopped at Mount Vernon, they got off. Mattie led them down a side street.

"In case the guards are looking for us," she said.

She stopped at a brick building topped by a clock tower. A statue of Benjamin Franklin marked the main entrance to the Pennsylvania house.

Then she saw two guards walking by.

"Quick," Mattie said. "In here."

Inside the Pennsylvania building, people were clustered in the middle of a huge round hall. The kids wriggled their way to the front. An enormous copper bell hung from a sturdy wood frame. The bell had a crack up one side.

"The Liberty Bell," said Mattie, awestruck. "It looks new!"

"It *is* new," said a man next to her. "It was made especially for the Exposition. The copper was donated from all over the country. They used Thomas Jefferson's kettle—"

"Thomas's kettle?" Sophie asked.

Mattie pulled Sophie and Alex back into the echoing hall.

"Did you hear that?" she said.

"I wonder why T.J.'s stuff is all over the place," Alex said. "Seems like Jefferson should have his own building."

"Maybe so, but we might find more of his things right here."

They wandered around the circular hall, peeking into various rooms. Most of them were furnished with paintings and chairs.

"Look!" said Alex. An old cracked bell hung above their heads. "I bet that's the *real* Liberty Bell."

They went into a large room where people milled around glass-topped display cases. Several sightseers examined a wooden chair.

Mattie read the plaque. "It's the chair Thomas Jefferson sat in when he wrote the Declaration of Independence!"

Alex waved her over to another display case. A gleaming sword shone like gold. "Jefferson's sword! Remember?"

Mattie nodded. "Thomas Jefferson pointed it at us on our very first trip back in time. And now it's at the world's fair. History really is weird."

Sophie was bent over a table, tugging on a strand of her blonde hair.

"What are you doing, Soph?" asked Alex.

"Seeing if my hair is this color."

Mattie wandered over to the small oval glass case. A strand of reddish hair was coiled inside.

"Thomas Jefferson had red hair," she said. "This is a lock of his hair!"

The kids strolled around, looking at other exhibits. Benjamin Franklin's lightning rod. John Quincy Adams's baby clothes. A painting of George Washington.

Mattie paused before a case containing a necklace made of shells. "This belonged to Pocahontas," she murmured.

Just then, a scream ripped through the great hall.

6

Gone!

"It's gone!" a woman shrieked.

Mattie rushed up to her. "What's gone?"

"I turned to tell my brother he must see President Jefferson's hair and—" The woman's hands fluttered.

Mattie looked down. The oval glass case containing Jefferson's hair was missing from the counter. She spun around, hoping to catch sight of the Man in White.

"I'm calling the guards," said the woman's brother, a man with a walrus mustache. He hurried to the exit.

Alex and Sophie ran over to Mattie.

"What's up?" Alex asked.

"The Jefferson Thief has struck again," Mattie replied. "I don't see him but I bet the Man in White is here somewhere."

"What did he take?" asked Alex.

"Jefferson's hair."

Mattie thought a moment. If she had just committed a crime, where would she go? The parlors? Or blend in with the ever-present crowd around the Liberty Bell?

"Alex," she said. "You and Soph check the sitting rooms. I'm going back to the main hall."

Mattie threaded her way through the crowd, but didn't see anyone dressed entirely in white.

Tweet! Tweeeeet!

A squad of Columbian Guards burst into the main hall. The man with the walrus mustache strode to meet them.

"Where's the robbery?" demanded a red-faced policeman. He spoke with a deep voice and flashed a gold badge. Mattie figured he was the chief.

"In here." Walrus Mustache led them to the exhibition room.

In minutes, Mattie knew, the guards would fan out all over the building. She had to find Alex and Sophie before they were spotted.

She scampered along the hall, peering into the sitting rooms. Finally, she found Alex and Sophie outside the Ladies' Parlor.

"The cops are here," she said. "We have to get out before they see us."

They were crossing the wide hall when

someone yelled, "Hey! That's those kids!"

"Keep walking," Mattie told the others. "Pretend you didn't hear. And *don't* run."

It was hard to saunter calmly toward the exit. Mattie kept her eyes straight ahead, but her heart was jumping like a rabbit in a basket.

"Police!" The chief's deep voice boomed behind them. "Stop, you three!"

"Now run!" Mattie tore through the door. Alex and Sophie were tight on her heels.

Tweeeeeeet! Tweet!

Boots stumped after them. Mattie risked a quick glance over her shoulder. The army of Columbian guards spilled through the door.

"Stop!" ordered Deep Voice. "Stop in the name of the law!"

People entering the Pennsylvania building stared. Mattie wondered when tourists would nab them.

She looked back to see if the guards were gaining. One of the policemen tripped over the curb. As he fell, he grabbed the arm of the guard next to him. Down they tumbled in a heap.

"Get up!" Deep Voice sounded angry. The two guards struggled to their feet and began to argue.

"Hurry!" Mattie said to Alex and Sophie. They raced down the street from the Pennsylvania building to the train station. Alex gave them fare money and they boarded just in time. A minute later, the train pulled out.

"We got away!" Alex said. "I bet those policemen are still fighting."

"No wonder so many purses are stolen around here," Mattie said. "Those guards are terrible."

"Do you still think the Man in White took

Jefferson's hair?" asked Alex. "We never did see him."

Mattie nodded. "I'm sure he's the Jefferson Thief."

"But how?" Alex asked. "How does he steal things with all those people around?"

"I don't know." Mattie sighed. How would they ever solve the mission or clear their names when they had to keep dodging the police?

Alex thought a moment. "If that guy likes Jefferson's stuff, how come he didn't take the spyglass?"

"Because we interrupted him. You took out our spyglass. Maybe he thought you beat him and stole Jefferson's spyglass first."

"He yelled for the guards and they're looking for us," Alex said. "Pretty smart."

"He wants the spyglass," Sophie said.

Mattie stared at her little sister. "Soph, you're right! Now would be the perfect time to steal it because the police are looking for *us*." She hopped off the bench.

"Where to now?" Alex asked.

"The Mount Vernon building."

They rode the train back to the state houses. Mount Vernon was jammed with tourists, but Mattie wiggled between them up the stairs to the second floor. She went straight to the table displaying Thomas Jefferson's belongings.

The brass tripod holding the spyglass was empty!

The others scooted up beside her.

"We're too late," Mattie said.

"Nobody's noticed the spyglass is missing yet," Alex said. "Which means he just took it."

"Look!" Sophie cried. "White!"

Mattie caught a glimpse of white before it faded into the mob. "That's him!" This time she was determined not to let him get away.

The Man in White heard her and whirled around. Mattie saw his look of surprise.

Then he melted into the crowd like hot butter.

"After him!" Mattie shouted.

They flew down the stairs and out the front door of Mount Vernon. The thief's white coat appeared and disappeared as it slithered in and out of view like a fish swimming between lily pads.

The kids raced after him through the streets of state houses, across lawns, past the lagoon and the Fisheries Building.

Mattie had a stitch in her side, but she didn't slow down. She was positive the Man in White had Thomas Jefferson's spyglass concealed inside his jacket. And the watch and lock of hair, too.

The kids whizzed past the Government Building, the Man in White only yards ahead of them. If they ran a little faster, Mattie thought, they could catch him.

The Jefferson Thief led them into the Court of Honor. The sun shone brightly against the white pavement and white buildings.

Sun-dazzled, Mattie blinked.

And in that instant, the Man in White vanished.

7

On Top
of the World

"How does he *do* that?" Mattie asked, spinning around.

"Maybe he's a magician," Alex said.

"He is," said Sophie.

But Mattie was thinking about something. In the Houdini Brothers's act, everyone wore black so they could blend in with the black cabinet. No one had noticed when Maria dropped the extra black bag behind the cabinet.

"He's like Maria!" she said suddenly.

Alex rolled his eyes. "I think the heat is getting to you."

"Remember how Maria and the others wore black clothes? They could do stuff and people wouldn't notice."

"I still don't get it," said Alex.

"The Man in White always runs away to the Court of Honor." Mattie twirled in a circle, arms outstretched. "Everything is white! He blends in with the white buildings."

"So how are we going to find him?"

A group of tourists strolled by just then. The women carried umbrellas, but the men wore blue-tinted glasses.

"Give me a quarter!" Mattie told Alex.

She raced over to a stall that sold the blue-tinted glasses. She grabbed a pair off the rack and slapped Alex's quarter on the counter.

Slipping the glasses on, she scanned the area. Against the white wall of the Electricity Building, she spied a pale blue figure carrying a silver-knobbed walking stick.

"There he is!" Mattie cried, pointing.

The Man in White turned sharply to see Mattie dashing toward him with Alex and Sophie not far behind. He scurried along the side of the white building, but Mattie kept track of him with her special glasses.

"He's going into the train station!" Alex said, gasping.

The Man in White swiveled through the turnstile, tossed a coin to the attendant, and hopped on the first car. The train chuffed, preparing to leave.

"Hurry!" Mattie yelled.

She pushed through the turnstile, waiting impatiently as Alex paid their fares, then leaped up the steps to the first car.

"Car's full, Miss," said the conductor. "Train's about to leave—"

Mattie sprinted back to the next car. No one barred her way, so she jumped on. She helped Sophie up the steps. Alex made it just as another conductor pulled the steps up. They found seats near the front.

"Watch for him to get off," Mattie told the others. "And be ready to run."

She didn't have to wait long. When the train stopped at the entrance to the Midway, the Man in White hurried off with a large group of passengers.

"There he is!" Alex exclaimed. "Let's go!"

They raced off the train and through the gate. The Midway was packed with tourists, donkeys, fruit carts, dancers, and street performers. Squealing bagpipes mingled with horns, flutes, whistles, drums, and gongs from every corner.

Mattie glimpsed a white coat among the shifting crowd. "Follow him!"

At that moment, a parade snaked down the street. A young boy in a red spangled costume rode in a carved sedan chair hefted by four turbaned men. People waved banners and flags. By the time the procession passed, the Man in White had vanished.

"He did it again!" Mattie cried.

They stood opposite the giant Ferris wheel. The great wheel slowed its revolution. The cars in front lowered toward the loading platform.

"If we're up high, we can see him," Alex said. "Like, as high as the Ferris wheel."

Mattie stared at him. "You don't mean—"

He nodded.

Mattie's heart skipped into her throat. "Alex, you know I'm afraid of heights!"

"You climbed the pea vine in our last adventure," he pointed out. "And that was way higher than this Ferris wheel."

"And I was petrified the whole time! I only did it to get Winchester back."

But she knew Alex was right. If they were going to catch the Jefferson Thief, they would have to be up high enough to spot him.

She sighed. "Buy our tickets before I change my mind."

In a flash, Alex purchased three tickets. They clicked through the turnstile and waited in a long line. The line moved quickly and soon the kids climbed the wide stairs to the loading platform.

As each train-like car stopped, passengers flowed out a door at one end, while new passengers boarded through the door at the far end. At last the kids were at the front of the line. When the next car descended, a man in a fancy uniform opened the door.

"All aboard, please," he said politely. "Kindly step to the far side of the car."

Mattie blinked in amazement. The floor was covered with a pink-flowered carpet. Wire-covered glass windows lined the length of the car. The ride was as fancy as a living room! She sat in one of the plush, round seats.

Alex and Sophie gazed out the window.

Mattie guessed at least fifty people sat in the rows of seats or stood by the windows.

A latch clicked and gears creaked. Mattie looked out the window at the people waiting for the next car. Then those people were gone and she was looking at the roof of the loading platform.

They were moving!

A teenage girl next to her whimpered, "I'm so frightened!"

Mattie closed her eyes. She'd only ridden a Ferris wheel once, at Olde Country Playworld. She remembered the sickening sway of the car.

"Mat!" Alex said in her ear. "It's okay."

Mattie opened her eyes. The car rocked gently. The teenage girl was eagerly taking in the view. People murmured with awe and delight as the car rose.

Alex prodded her. "C'mon, we've got to look for the Man in White before he gets away."

Mattie joined him and Sophie at the window. Below, the Midway villages shrank until they were the size of dollhouses. As the wheel turned, the car grew farther from the ground. The great white buildings in the Court of Honor were no bigger than Monopoly houses. Beyond, Lake Michigan glimmered a deep blue.

"Do you see him?" Mattie asked Alex and Sophie.

"People are little like ants," Sophie remarked.

"Wait till we start back down," Alex said.

The wheel began its final revolution.

Mattie stared at several white blotches inside a fence. Then she realized the white blotches were ostriches. Outside the fence, a man wearing all white was stuffing objects into a satchel.

"It's him!" she exclaimed. "He's at the ostrich farm!"

Alex clutched the brass rail. "I hope he stays put till the ride is over."

Mattie thought of something. "Even if we find him again, we can't catch him by ourselves. We need help."

"Harry will help us," Sophie said.

"Great idea, Soph!" Alex said. "We're closer to the Dime Museum than that ostrich place."

At last the car settled gently by the platform. The attendant announced, "All out, please."

Mattie, Alex and Sophie bolted from the

car. They raced down the steps of the platform and across the Midway to the Dime
Museum.

Harry was outside, drinking lemonade.

"Hey, kids," he said. "Where's the fire?"

Mattie clutched his sleeve. "We need your
help! The police think we stole Thomas Jefferson's watch and spyglass. But we know who
really did it. Can you catch him?"

"Where is he?" Harry Houdini asked.

"By the big birds," Sophie replied.

"The ostrich farm? Give me one second."
Harry disappeared into the museum. He
returned with a length of rope. "Let's go."

The kids ran toward the ostrich farm, but
Harry Houdini sped past them. Mattie had
never seen anyone run so fast!

The Man in White was still by the ostrich
farm fence. When he saw Harry and the kids, he

took off into the crowd, clutching the satchel.

Harry caught him before the man had run three feet. He tackled the white-suited man, bringing him to the pavement.

"All right, sport," Harry said. "The game's over."

"Get off me!" The Man in White's face turned red. "I'll have you arrested!"

"I don't think so." Harry pulled the man's hands behind him and began binding them with the rope. "The last person you want is a policeman."

"You'll pay!" the man yelled. "My lawyer will put you in jail!"

Harry stood and spoke to the kids. "I'll go fetch the guards. You stay here. He won't untie my knots, don't worry."

Then the magician sprinted through the crowd. Bystanders gawked.

"Where's Jefferson's watch?" Mattie asked the Man in White. "And his spyglass?"

He glowered at her. "Be quiet, you rude girl."

"Who are you calling rude?"

"He's getting loose," Sophie said.

The Man in White suddenly whipped his arms around, letting the rope fall. He flexed his wrists, grinning. "Mr. Houdini isn't as good as he thinks."

Mattie stared at him. "How did you do that? Those knots were tied by a magician!"

Then she remembered what Sophie had said earlier. The Man in White wasn't an ordinary thief.

He was a magician, too!

8

Bending the Rule

Mattie felt her face flush with anger. He was not getting away again! She leaped onto his back. Alex tackled the man, too.

The Man in White tumbled to the ground with a grunt.

"Let me up!" he demanded. Mattie was surprised at his strength.

She and Alex couldn't hold him much longer. And the guards might be having trouble finding them.

"Sophie!" she said. "Cry! Really loud!"

Sophie opened her mouth wide. "Aiiiiiiiiieeeeeeeee!"

Her wail rose above the gongs and pipes and drums. It drowned out the singing and chanting. Mattie was proud of her little sister. Nobody could cry like Sophie!

Within seconds, Harry Houdini and four guards pushed through the crowds.

"What's all this commotion?" a big-nosed policeman asked.

Harry stood over the Man in White. "You got free of my knots but you couldn't shake these kids, could you, Jack?"

Big Nose jerked the Man in White up by one arm. "Well, if it isn't Jack Langtree. How many pocketbooks did you swipe today?"

"He took more than that," Mattie said. "He

stole Thomas Jefferson's watch and spyglass. Look in that bag."

The guard emptied the satchel on the pavement. Out fell wallets, purses, a silver watch, a spyglass, and a small case holding a lock of reddish hair.

"He tried to make it look like we took those things," Alex said.

Big Nose nodded. "We have been searching for three kids and you three fit the description."

"Now you know who really did it," said Mattie.

Big Nose shook his finger at him. "I see you've graduated from purse-snatching to robbery."

"That guy's a magician, isn't he?" Mattie asked Harry.

"Yes, but a bad one," Harry replied. "He

uses his skills to pick pockets and swipe small items, like from the exhibits."

One of the guards latched handcuffs around Jack Langtree's wrists.

Big Nose held up the spyglass and watch. "What were you planning to do with these?" he asked Langtree.

"Sell them, what else?" Jack Langtree raised his chin, as if he had done nothing wrong. "I know a collector in New York City who will pay a lot of money for anything owned by Thomas Jefferson."

"Langtree and I once performed in the same theater," Harry said. "He was jealous of my act."

"You think you're so great," Langtree sneered. "I caught your act earlier, Ehrich Weiss. I don't see people packing the house."

Ehrich Weiss, Mattie thought. That must

be Houdini's real name. She remembered the message on their postcard. It was signed by "E.W." And "pack the house" was show business talk.

"People will come to see the good magician!" said Sophie. "Not the bad one."

Onlookers chuckled. One man said to his wife, "Let's go see the *good* magician."

Harry grinned. "I guess I'd better get back to Kohl's. It's almost time for our next show."

Mattie, Alex, and Sophie walked with Harry back to the Dime Museum.

"Did you hear those people? They're all coming to your show," Mattie said.

"I hope you're right," said Harry.

At the Dime Museum, the kids waited eagerly inside the entrance, counting each new customer.

"That guy and that lady just went in," Mattie

said to Alex. "How many does that make?"

"Thirty-seven."

"Thirty-seven! Is that all?"

Sophie peeked through the double doors. "Harry and Theo are going to start."

"Let's go sit down," said Alex.

The entire front row was vacant, so the kids sat in the middle where they had the best view. When the red velvet curtains swished up, Harry and Theo stood on either side of the black-painted cabinet, as before.

Mattie saw Harry's gray eyes flick around the half-empty theater. She wondered if he was disappointed.

If he was, it didn't show in his performance. Harry was locked in the trunk and Theo stepped behind the cabinet's curtain. Then Harry reappeared in his brother's place so fast, Mattie thought they were the same person for a second.

She applauded louder than Alex. "Bravo!" she called.

"Gravy!" Sophie shouted, clapping Ellsworth's feet together. Mattie and Alex giggled.

Harry Houdini stepped forward with Theo in a low bow. When Harry straightened up, his eyes met Mattie's and he winked. The curtain dropped.

Mattie turned to Alex. "We didn't get crowds of people to come to Harry's show. Now he'll go back to New York. We didn't accomplish our mission."

"He goes back to New York anyway," Alex told her. "It was in the TV show, remember?"

"Then why were we sent here?" Mattie asked, confused. "If we were supposed to help Harry Houdini, why didn't we get sent to another time in his life?"

"We showed him he is the best magician," Alex said. "But maybe he needs us to tell him he'll be really famous."

"We can't change history!"

"He *will* be famous," said Alex. "What's wrong with telling him?"

Mattie chewed her bottom lip. She wished the Travel Guides gave them *rules*. Like what to do and what not to do when they traveled back in time.

"Okay," she said. "Let's go backstage. But *don't* give Harry ideas."

They found Harry and Theo sitting on the trunk outside their dressing room.

Harry had something in his hands, but he put it down when he saw them.

"Hey, kids," he said. "What did you think of the show?"

"Terrific!" Alex put in.

Harry snorted. "Glad you think so. Doesn't seem like anybody else does."

"We're heading home at the end of the week," said Theo.

"You'll get another job," Mattie told Harry. "Better than this one. People will come from miles to see you. The Houdini name will be known far and wide."

Harry stared at Mattie. "You talk like you can read the future. You know what? I believe you!" He laughed.

"We have to be going now," Mattie said.

"Thanks for showing me the coin trick," said Alex.

Harry walked with them to the entrance, carrying a pair of handcuffs.

"What are you doing with those?" Mattie asked, shooting Alex a meaningful glance.

"Just fooling around," Harry replied. "I'm very good at getting out of handcuffs. It's not a trick. I can get out of any handcuffs in the world."

At the door, the kids hesitated.

"Goodbye," Harry told them. "Have a safe journey back home."

Sophie held up her stuffed elephant. "Ellsworth says you could make an elephant disappear in one of your tricks."

Mattie elbowed her sister. "Don't give him any more ideas!"

Harry laughed but Mattie saw the glint in his gray eyes.

Night had fallen over the fairgrounds. The Ferris wheel turned slowly, twinkling with thousands of lights.

"Do we have to go home?" asked Sophie.

"Yeah," Alex said. "Do we have to go home now?"

Just then a red, white, and blue flower erupted overhead in a glittery shower. Fireworks exploded over the Grand Basin. The kids looked up as the sky rained stars.

"Looks like the Fourth of July," said Alex.

"We have our own fireworks waiting for us at home," Mattie said. "Guess we'd better go back."

"Now?" Alex asked. "In the middle of all these people?"

"No one will notice us go. They're all busy watching the fireworks. It's the art of misdirection, remember?"

Alex grinned. He took the spyglass from his pocket and held on to one end. Sophie gripped the middle. Mattie closed her eyes and clutched the other end of the spyglass.

Her feet *whooshed* from beneath her.

Thump!

Her feet hit the tower room floor. Mattie opened her eyes. Alex and Sophie appeared beside her.

Outside, the sun was shining brightly. It was still morning.

"Another mission accomplished," said Alex.

"I'm not so sure," said Mattie.

"You made Harry feel better, even though he went home," said Alex.

Mattie nodded. "I guess we can bend the rule once in a while. For a good reason."

She walked over to the desk, opened the bottom drawer, and removed an envelope. As she closed the drawer, her fingers trailed over the worn wood. She thought about what Ms. Pettibone-Shute had said about furniture making journeys. She wondered what stories their desk would tell if it could talk.

"I'm hungry," Alex said. "Let's take the Travel Guide's letter downstairs and raid the kitchen."

Alex opened the bookcase-panel and crawled through. Mattie got down on her hands and knees to follow. Then she noticed Sophie standing by the desk.

"Soph, we're leaving."

"Coming," said Sophie.

Mattie turned away, but not before she saw Sophie reach into the pocket of her sundress and drop a pinch of something glittery into one of the desk drawers.

It looked like—no, it couldn't be . . . diamond dust?

Dear Mattie, Alex, and Sophie:

I hope you enjoyed the World's Columbian Exposition. Alex, you finally got to ride on the first—and biggest—Ferris wheel in history. And Mattie, you are getting better about high places!

You only visited a small part of the fair. But you saw how vast it was. People living in the mid—19th century, and into the 20th century, traveled to world's fairs for a once—in—a—lifetime experience.

The fairs were held in different countries. Each country tried to make their fair the biggest and most important by building something fantastic.

So what was so great about this world's fair? It was America's party, a celebration that lasted from May to October, 1893.

Built in Chicago, the fair was nicknamed

"The White City" because many of the buildings were white. One young man, L. Frank Baum, visited the White City and later wrote about the Emerald City in his books about Oz

Many new inventions were introduced at the fair, such as elevators, electric boats, elevated electric trains, and moveable sidewalks. The famous inventor, Thomas Edison, showed his "kinetograph," which was the world's first movie projector.

The Midway was also a new idea. For the first time, people could walk down a long avenue with rides, shows, food, and other forms of entertainment. Modern-day carnivals grew from the Midway.

And what about the "World's Greatest Ride?" At another world's fair, the 1889 Paris Exposition, the Eiffel Tower was the centerpiece. America wanted an engineering marvel bigger and better at their fair. George Ferris, a bridge builder from Pennsylvania, created the Great Wheel. Many people didn't think it would work.

The wheel stood 264 feet high, with a diameter of 250 feet. The 70-ton axle was 45 feet long. This single piece of steel could hold 1,200 tons! People flocked to ride in one of the 36 cars. In 1906, the Great Wheel was destroyed. But today you can find a Ferris wheel much like the Great Wheel at carnivals and fairs everywhere.

Mattie, you were right about the popcorn Theo Houdini gave you. It was indeed Cracker Jack, though it wasn't called that until after 1900. Other foods first tasted at the fair were Shredded Wheat cereal, Juicy Fruit chewing gum, and chili con carne.

The Columbian Exposition may have been one of the first places Harry Houdini performed. Harry was born Ehrich Weiss on April 6, 1874, in Budapest, Hungary. He moved to the United States when he was young, first living in Wisconsin, then New York City.

Harry caught the performing "bug" early. Around age nine, he put on a trapeze act. When he was sixteen, Harry got a job in a necktie factory. In his spare time, he swam, boxed, and ran ten miles a day. He met Jacob Hyman at the necktie factory and they put together a magic act. "Ehrie" called himself Harry Houdini. When Jacob left, Harry's brother Theo took his place.

After performing at the 1893 World's Fair, Harry met Bess Rahner and they were married. Bess became Harry's partner. After working dime museums and small clubs, Harry added handcuffs to the act. He became "King of the Handcuffs," able to escape handcuffs, leg irons, and shackles.

Harry Houdini became an escape artist, freeing himself from locked boxes, even underwater. He even made an elephant vanish. Wearing a giant wristwatch, an elephant called Jenny walked into a huge cabinet. Two seconds later, Houdini opened the curtain. Jenny was gone!

Harry Houdini died in 1926, on Halloween, from complications of appendicitis.

I'm glad you were able to take part in America's celebration. Your next adventure will take you to a time when America was not celebrating. Think "brother against brother."

Yours in time,

"Ms. Pettibone-Shute"

TIME SPIES MISSION NO. 4:
LEARN THE ART OF MISDIRECTION

Harry Houdini said the secret to magic is misdirection. The secret to spying is also misdirection. By doing one thing to distract people, you can actually be doing something else. Until your next adventure, learn this magic trick to help you or a fellow spy get out of a tight spot.

WHAT YOU NEED:
A nickel or other small coin

WHAT YOU DO:

1. Hold the nickel in your right hand, between your thumb and index finger. Your hand is straight. The palm of your hand should face your body.

2. Practice passing the nickel from your right hand to your left hand. Practice a lot so you can fake this well.

3. When you are ready to perform the trick, pretend to grab the nickel with your left hand.

4. Let the nickel drop into your right hand.

5. Pretend to fling the coin in the air with your left hand. You made the coin "disappear!"

TIM

"A time-traveling mystery . . . that will keep kids turning the pages!"
—Marcia T. Jones,
co-author of *The Bailey School Kids*

Give an important message to General Washington in
Secret in the Tower

Catch a dinosaur thief in
Bones in the Badlands

Climb into the pages of *Jack and the Beanstalk* in
Giant in the Garden

Help legendary magician Harry Houdini in
Magician in the Trunk

Reunite a Civil War spy with his brother in
Signals in the Sky
MAY 2007

Unmask the Headless Horseman in
Rider in the Night
AUG 2007

Save the Race of the Century in
Horses in the Wind
NOV 2007

For more information visit:
www.timespies.com